THE
FIELD DAY
FROM THE
BLACK LAGOON

Get more monster-sized laughs from

The Black Lagoon:

THE
FIELD DAY
FROM THE
BLACK LAGOON

3-LEGGED RACE

by Mike Thaler
Illustrated by Jared Lee

SCHOLASTIC INC.

New York   Toronto   London   Auckland   Sydney
Mexico City   New Delhi   Hong Kong   Buenos Aires

To Jan and Sylvia,
true brother and sister
open hearts — open arms
—M.T.

To my best man,
Larry Fasse
—J.L.

No part of this publication may be reproduced, stored in a retrieval system, or transmitted in any form or by any means, electronic, mechanical, photocopying, recording, or otherwise, without written permission of the publisher. For information regarding permission, write to Scholastic Inc., Attention: Permissions Department, 557 Broadway, New York, NY 10012.

ISBN-13: 978-0-439-68076-9
ISBN-10: 0-439-68076-X

20 19 18   11 12 13/0
                                                          40
Printed in the U.S.A.
First printing, April 2005

CONTENTS

BUG, HALF AWAKE.

"SPEEDY" THE PIG →

CHAPTER 1
THE AGONY OF DA-FEET

COACH KONG.

Coach Kong marches us into the gym and lines us up. He paces back and forth, holding his clipboard. "Next Friday, we're having a field day," he declares.

He reads off some of the events from his list. I nervously start picking at the rubber on my sneakers. It sounds like the script for an action movie.

"Parachute," says Coach Kong.

Do we have to jump out of an airplane?

GET THE LEAD OUT!

EVENTS
1.
2.
3.

"Obstacle course," he continues. Do we have to run through fire, leap over lions, hop over hippos, skip through snakes, and tiptoe around tigers?

Then there's Charlie Over the Water. They fill a big tank with hungry sharks and throw us in. That gets you ready for the One-Legged Race.

I don't think I *field* so good. I ask Coach Kong if everyone has to be at the field day. He just laughs and says, "It'll be a day you'll never forget."

CHAPTER 2
LAUNCH TIME

At lunch, we eat big bean burritos and look over the stuff to do at next Friday's field day event. There's the Bean Bag Toss. That should be easy—we just ate 'em.

There's another event called Scarf Tag. Eric says they should make an event called Barf Tag because it would be so cool and gross. Some of the girls move to another table. It's so easy to make them queasy!

BARF BAG
(KEEP COOL)

← THIS SIDE UP.

We read off another one, Three-Legged Race—that should require major surgery. OUCH!

Then there's the Tug-of-War. This is going to be survival of the fittest. I don't fit at all.

STATION 1

STATION 2

Who knows? Maybe I'll win the Sack Race. I am a good sleeper.

Penny and Doris say that they will luck out and win a bunch of events like Jump Rope, Hula-Hoop, and Egg Race.

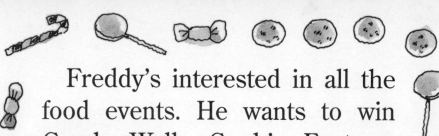

Freddy's interested in all the food events. He wants to win Candy Walk, Cookie Factory, and Bubble Gum. He's starting to train right now by seeing how many pieces of bubble gum he can fit in his mouth at the same time. By the time the bell rings, he's up to eleven.

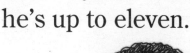

I LOVE THIS EVENT.

PICKLE

CHAPTER 3
OLYM-PICKLES

On the way home, all the kids are talking about the field day. Freddy says it's just like the Olympics. That's right, I think—we'll all *limp* home.

"I'm a good jumper," brags Derek.

"I'm a good bumper," blurts Freddy.

"I'm fast," declares Randy.

"I'm last," I sigh.

OOPS!

13

For the rest of the way home, Eric and I discuss the situation. There's not going to be even one video game—bummer! So we're going to have to get into shape.

But what shape should we get into? Square, round, triangular? Eric says, "Muscles . . . we need muscles . . . FAST!"

"What about clams?" I ask. "Do we need clams, too?"

He rolls his eyes and says, "We have to get fit, Hubie."

"To fit what?" I ask.

Eric says that he's going to get fit, and I should shape up. It's all too confusing. I just stare out the window and count red convertibles.

RED

THERE'S ONE.

SCHOOL BUS

CHAPTER 4
MUSCLE-BOUND

AWESOME!

When I get home, I realize Eric had a point, and it wasn't just the top of his head. I need some muscles ... quick, if I want to win any events.

I EAT MUSCLES.

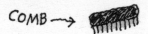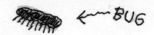
On TV that night, there's an ad for muscles. It's a complete body-building system for $19.95. Normally, it sells for $385. But if you call in the next five minutes, they'll cut the price in half to $9.97.

It's called Wimpflex and it guarantees muscles in eight days or your money back.

The field day is in six days. Maybe I could go from total wimp to almost wonderful. I check my piggy bank. I have ten dollars—I'm on my way—I call in. Look out, field day, here I come!

I send off my money and wait. Every day I check the mailbox after school. Days pass. I'm getting weaker and weaker. Then three days later, it comes!

My complete Wimpflex body-building system. I eagerly open the little box. It's a rubber band and a booklet. Well, I read the booklet and start right away to make up for lost time. Maybe I can go from shrimp to strong-man before the field day.

19

CHAPTER 5
MY PER-PLEX MACHINE

The first exercise is for abs. What's an ab?

It says, "Lie down." That's easy. I can do that. Then it says, "Sit up." I just lay down and got comfortable, why would I sit up?

STEP 1

STEP 2

STEP 3

REPEAT STEP 1

BICEPS

ABS

I move on to the next section. It says, "Biceps." Do I have to buy something else? There's a picture of an arm. Okay, it says, "Put your Wimpflex around a door handle and pull." It's a silly way to open the door, but I'll try it. While I'm pulling, Mom opens the door, and my rubber band snaps. I go flying across the room.

Well, so much for biceps. Maybe I won't need 'em for field day.

SNAP!

WIMP

The next exercise is for pecs, and the one after that is for thighs. I think this is a body-building system for chickens. I want my money back.

I phone the number on the booklet. A man answers. I tell him that I'm not satisfied. He says that my Wimpflex is

SUPER CHICKEN

PECS

THIGHS

guaranteed to give me muscles. Then he asks if I'm holding up the phone.

HELLO.

I say, "Yes."

He says that if I'm holding the phone, I have muscles, and then I hear a click. I look at my $9.97 rubber band and start to feel sad. I just got conned!

WIMPFLEX

CLICK!

WIMP DOG

CHAPTER 6
A HEALTHY ATTITUDE

The next day, Mom tells me that walking is the best exercise. I can walk, so I am in good shape.

She also says that a well-balanced diet is important.

She claims, "You are what you eat."

So I ask for a hot dog. I'd like to be a hot dog at the field day.

HOT DOG

COLD DOG

Later that day, I go to the health food store. The shelves are loaded with products and promises. Power Powder says that it can give you a healthier body in three days. Another is called Energizer—I don't want to eat a battery, though. There is even some stuff called Muscle Maker and another thing called Puny Pills. I don't think I want any of them.

GRRRRRR

CATTAILS

25

I walk farther into the store and there's row after row of powders, pills, and potions that all say they are packed with power.

Each one promises a healthier body in three minutes or three days.

There are Brawn Bars, Force Flakes, and Tower Tabs that strengthen, invigorate, and fortify.

IF YOU TAKE ONE OF THESE A DAY YOU'LL LOOK LIKE ME.

POWER GUY PRODUCTS

POWER GUY

COOL.

There's another product called Lightning Bar—one bite will turn you into an Olympic champion and two bites will give you the power to fly. I don't think there's a flying competition at the field day.

Another aisle contains a whole alphabet of vitamins and minerals. And all the store's signs say that you need to buy them all.

AWESOME.

Then there's a weird food area. Hot dogs made from cereal. Cereal made from seaweed. Then there's tofu, which sounds like it comes from in between your toes. GROSS! And it's all really, really expensive.

I wonder if they'd like to buy my rubber band.

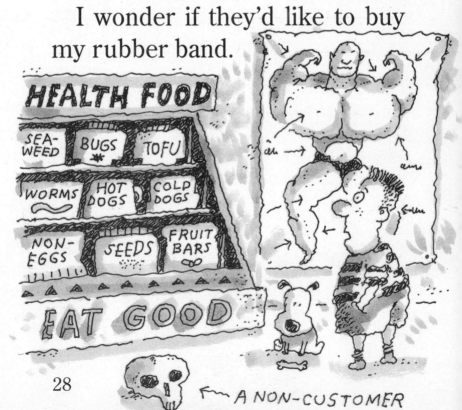

HEALTH FOOD

SEA-WEED BUGS TOFU

WORMS HOT DOGS COLD DOGS

NON-EGGS SEEDS FRUIT BARS

EAT GOOD

A NON-CUSTOMER

CHAPTER 7
PICK ON ME!

I'm in training. I mean I played with my electric train for hours. Nobody at school notices my new muscles, but I know they're under my shirt somewhere.

Coach Kong says it's time to choose teams for tomorrow's field day.

DOLLAR → [image: dollar bill] ← BAD FOR FLIPPING.

Eric and Derek are the captains. We all line up and they flip a coin to see who goes first. Eric wins and picks Freddy, who now can get twenty-six pieces of bubble gum into his mouth. I flex my bicep, but Derek picks Randy because he's the fastest kid in class. Then I flex my abs, and Eric picks me because he's my best friend.

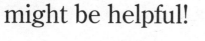

That just leaves Doris and Penny. Doris weighs more than Penny, so we could use her as an anchor for our team. Well, Derek picks her, and Penny joins our team. She's very thin. Maybe we could use her as a rope—that might be helpful!

I wish Superman or The Hulk was on our team. Oh well, we'll have to do our best without them.

After school, I ride my bike to a local gym. Standing by the door, I watch other people work out. Boy, they sweat a lot. They smell, too! YUCK!

Then I ride over to the health food store and breathe in the air. I hope some of it will make me healthier and stronger.

I'm doing everything I can do to get into shape.

I even read my Wimpflex booklet over again. I hope that is some sort of exercise. Afterward, I watch a bodybuilding movie and pray that my muscles can see how rock-hard they should be. I hope that I am ready for tomorrow.

CHAPTER 8
DOOM AND GLOOM

Later that night, I have a nightmare—well, it's more like a field-mare. YIKES!

It's tomorrow, and the field day has started. . . .

Derek, Randy, and Doris have all grown into ten-foot-tall giants. Coach Kong has joined their team as well. They even have team uniforms and a team name—THE GIANTS.

← NIGHTMARE

Eric, Freddy, Penny, and I are called the Wimps. Boy, I wish I had my rubber band.

The first event is the Tug-of-War. Our team holds on tightly to the rope. The Giants give one yank and we go sailing over the school!

The next event is the Soccer Kick. They kick us instead of the ball. And we go sailing over the school again!

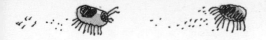

After that, the Bean Bag Toss starts. But the Giants toss us. Once again, we go sailing over the school.

The last event is Bubble Gum Blowout. Freddy is now able to get 240 pieces of bubble gum into his mouth.

Then he blows a gigantic bubble. It gets bigger and bigger. He begins to float up.

We grab on to him and together we all sail over the school. Our team is disqualified for leaving the playing field.

39

SON → SUN →

I wake up and I've fallen out of bed . . . right into Friday. It's time for the field day! Hope our team's ready.

CHAPTER 9
LET THE GAMES BEGIN

On the bus to school, everyone is bragging. My team and Derek's team are both bursting with boasts and insults:

"We're better . . . you're butter," they yell.

"Oh yeah, we're champs," we reply. "You're chumps."

BUTTER   BUTTERFLY

WINNER→ THANK YOU. WHINER→ I WAS TRIPPED.

"Oh yeah, we're winners," they reply. "You're whiners."

Wow, that one kind of stung.

"Whatever, we're number one and you're done," our team yells out.

42

"All of you cut that out," says Mr. Fenderbender, the school bus driver. "It's not whether you win or lose . . . It's how you play the game."

"That's right," says Eric. "And we'll play it better than Derek's team."

"I don't think so," says Derek. "Because we're going to crush you. Then mush you. And afterward turn you into slush!"

The funny thing is, we were all good friends yesterday, before we chose teams.

CHAPTER 10
FIELD OF BATTLE

Well, we survive the trip to school, but now no one's talking to one another. We're all finely tuned athletes focused on the challenges that lie before us. I feel like we're at the Olympic Games, marching out onto the field of battle.

I knew I should have bought a Lightning Bar so I could fly away. Too late for that. As we arrive at station number one, the Basketball Shoot, Coach Kong is standing with his clipboard.

"Okay," he says. "What are the team names?"

Derek shouts out, "The Tigers!"

Coach writes it down and turns to us.

STATION 1
BASKETBALL SHOOT

47

Oh my gosh, Eric and I didn't know that we had to have a team name. We both look at each other.

Then Penny shouts out, "The Pussycats."

Coach Kong writes it down.

"Meow," snickers Derek.

"This could be cat-astrophic," shouts Eric.

Then Coach Kong gives out the basketballs. He hands one to

MEOW.

Penny. She's our best free shooter. Sure enough, she all of her baskets.

Derek doesn't get any in misses the backboard completely. We win the event and we put our best paw forward.

THUD!

I MISSED!

COOL.

Station number two is the Three-Legged Race. Coach ties my leg to Eric's and then ties Derek's to Randy's. Then he yells, "On your mark, get set, go!"

We're off and hobbling. I don't know how spiders walk with eight legs. Our legs get tangled, and we fall over. It's obvious Derek and Randy have been practicing, because they win by two noses.

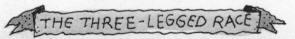

DIRECTIONS

① CHOOSE SOMEBODY YOU LIKE.

② TIE YOUR MIDDLE LEGS TOGETHER.

③ PUT YOUR LEFT ARM AROUND YOUR PARTNER.

④ TOGETHER, MOVE YOUR LEFT LEG FORWARD, THEN YOUR RIGHT.

⑤ REPEAT UNTIL YOU CROSS THE FINISH LINE.

ROPE

THE THREE-LEGGED RACE

We're tied, one to one. Next is the Water Balloon Toss, and Derek's team drowns. They lose with a big splash! Our team floats to the top with a win.

CIRCLE THE DOG THAT'S → DIFFERENT.

We're ahead two to one, but then they catch up in the Ring Toss. Randy is a ringer. I didn't know he was so good. But we pull ahead with a Hula-Hoop victory. Penny out-wiggles Doris. She's really hip!

53

The Tigers catch up in the Bean Bag Toss. And we have our first casualty. Eric gets beaned with a bag and has to go see Miss Hearse. Derek calls Eric a beanie baby as he leaves the field.

After a few minutes, Eric's back out on the field in a flash. He's hopping mad for the Sack Race. We bounce back into the lead by sacking them with a win.

But then the Tigers give us the boot and win the Soccer Kick contest. Now we're all tied up again going into the Bubble Gum blowout.

CHAPTER 11
A BLOWOUT

Our hopes are riding on Freddy, who can now get twenty-nine pieces of bubble gum into his mouth. Eric and I keep shoving it in until his cheeks are puffed out like softballs.

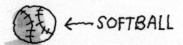 ←SOFTBALL

When he tries to blow, Freddy just starts turning an odd shade of blue and we have to rush him to Miss Hearse, who does an emergency extraction with pliers. Derek's team wins the event, and our whole team is blue.

STAY BACK. GIVE HIM SOME AIR.

MY HAND IS STUCK!

NURSE, WILL HE BE OK?

HE'LL BE FINE.

But we rally and take the Cake Walk.

It's tied again! Now it's all riding on the last event—the Tug-of-War. Can we pull it off?

Freddy, who still is a shade of aqua, is our anchor. The Tigers' anchor is Doris. She looks pretty tough. We line up on the rope and spit on our hands. We're off!

We huff and puff. We tug and chug. We yank and crank. We heave and haul, but nobody's budging at all—not even an inch!

60

IF 15 MINUTES HAVE PAST, HOW MANY MINUTES ARE LEFT IN AN HOUR? ANSWER ON PAGE 64.

TICK
TICK
TICK

After fifteen minutes of major exertion, Coach Kong blows his whistle, and he declares the field day a tie. We let go of the rope and all fall down laughing and rolling around. Everyone's beat, but a winner!

61

CHAPTER 12
HAPPY ENDING

So we all get to celebrate because we're all field day champs. As a reward, each of us gets a Popsicle and a gold medal. Well, not really gold, more like yellow cardboard medals made by Miss Swamp.

MISS SWAMP, THE ART TEACHER.

But we wear our medals with pride on the bus ride home and talk all about what a great time we had at the field day.

The field day totally rocked! Then we all laugh together, remembering all the fun stuff that had nothing to do with winning, like the water balloons bursting and the look on Freddy's face when he tried to blow a bubble.

When I get home, I find my rubber band and throw it in the trash. I don't need a gimmick to be a winner!

Maybe next year for the field day, I'll start exercising more and be as big as Mr. Universe. Well, maybe that's stretching it a little. At least I know that it'll be a field day of fun.

HUBIE NEXT YEAR... (MAYBE).